Jacqui Farley

Daisy Bones and the Mummy's Finger

Illustrated by Jamie Smith

Macdonald Young Books

Class No. _____ J _____   Acc No. C/134924

Author: Farley, J   Loc:- 5 JUN 2003

LEABHARLANN
CHONDAE AN CHABHAIN

1. **This book may be kept three weeks. It is to be returned on / before the last date stamped below.**
2. **A fine of 25c will be charged for every week or part of week a book is overdue.**

0 8 AUG 2003		
1 2 SEP 2003		
1 9 SEP 2003		
22 April		

For Tony and Dane

Text copyright © Jacqui Farley 1997
Illustrations copyright © Jamie Smith 1997

First published in Great Britain in 1997
by Macdonald Young Books
61 Western Road
Hove
East Sussex
BN3 1JD

The right of Jacqui Farley to be identified as the author
of this Work and the right of Jamie Smith to be
identified as the illustrator of this Work has been
asserted by them in accordance with the Copyright,
Designs and Patents Act 1988.

Designed and Typeset by Backup Creative Service, Dorset DT10 1DB
Printed and bound in Belgium by Proost International Book Production

British Library Cataloguing in Publication Data available

ISBN 0 7500 2313 9
ISBN 0 7500 2314 7 (pb)

Chapter One

On a Thursday morning in June, a school party was touring a museum.

"Drone, drone," Mrs Hoskins, the teacher, waffled on. "Drone, drone."

Weasel yawned.

"Wake up!" hissed Daisy. "We'll be at the ancient Egyptian exhibit in a minute. You'll miss the mummies."

Daisy Bones was not an ordinary girl. To begin with, she was much cleverer than most adults, teachers included. She didn't like pop music or dolls. She liked detective stories and was often found with her nose rammed in a book, where it usually stayed until the last page had been read.

Her best friend was Weasel, a nickname he got on his first day at school because he looked like one! They became friends when Daisy moved next door and stayed friends because Daisy said every great detective had a sidekick and Weasel could be hers. Being Daisy Bones' sidekick was never dull.

"Look at that!" cried Weasel excitedly, looking at a glass display case. "They can even tell you what that mummy had for its last meal."

"Fascinating," said Daisy. "I wonder how that got in there?"

"What got in where?" asked Weasel.

"There's a ham sandwich beside that mummy," said Daisy. "I'm pretty certain they didn't have ham sandwiches in ancient Egypt."

"It says on our worksheet to look for something unusual about one of the mummies. I bet this is it!"

"No, I think it must be the one with the missing finger over there."

"Then how did a ham sandwich get inside the case?"

"Oh, whoever examined the contents of the stomach must have left their lunch there by accident."

Daisy wandered off towards another exhibit.

Chapter Two

The children ate their packed lunches in a special room for school parties. Daisy enjoyed hers, but Weasel didn't fancy his much. He kept looking at *his* ham sandwich and thinking about the one with the mummy. Yuck!

After lunch, an important looking lady came and had a serious talk with Mrs Hoskins. The lady was quite angry and waved her arms about a lot. Mrs Hoskins went very red in the face and turned towards her class.

"This is the curator. She has something to ask you," she snapped. "And there'll be trouble if any of you have been up to mischief."

"Something has gone missing from one of the display cases in the Egyptian exhibit," said the curator crossly. "If it is not returned immediately, I will call the police."

"No one could be *that* hungry," whispered Weasel with a shudder, still thinking about the ham sandwich.

"What's missing?" asked Daisy Bones.

"A mummy's finger," said the curator.

"I see," said Daisy Bones. "Why do you think we'd steal a mummy's finger?"

"As a prank, of course," said the curator impatiently. "Now, we will all return to the Egyptian exhibit and turn our backs. Then the culprit can return the finger and no more will be said. Come along, children."

A very insulted class followed the curator and Mrs Hoskins back to the exhibit.

Everyone turned their backs and waited. Nothing happened. Then Mrs Hoskins made them all empty their pockets. There was some bubble gum, marbles, a few sweets, but no mummified fingers.

"See," said Mrs Hoskins triumphantly. "My pupils are not thieves!"

The children were ushered back into the lunch room and the police were called. The curator was sure they had pinched the mummy's finger. The fact that there was no proof wouldn't convince her.

Chapter Three

While Mrs Hoskins was busy arguing with
the curator about missing the coach and
having to be back at school for three
o'clock, Daisy Bones and Weasel slipped
out of the lunch room and made their way
back to the Egyptian exhibit.

"I want to have a closer look at the
mummy with the missing finger," said
Daisy to Weasel.

They looked at the mummy's hands, which were crossed on its chest. Daisy walked around the cabinet until she came to a small hole that had been cut in the glass. She peered inside.

"Hey look at this!" said Daisy excitedly.

At the base of the missing finger was a small ink mark.

"Is there a fingerprint?" asked Weasel.

"No, I think whoever took the finger used an ink pen nib to prise it off."

"What are you children doing in here?"

They spun round to find a police officer and a man in a smart suit.

"We were looking for clues," said Daisy. "What are *you* doing here?"

"I'm Detective Inspector Lard, I'm supposed to be here," said the Detective Inspector. "Constable, detain those children."

"You can't detain us, we've discovered vital evidence," said Daisy Bones.

The Detective Inspector looked over her shoulder at the inky mark on the mummy's hand.

"Hmm, looks like someone used an ink pen nib to break off the finger," said Detective Inspector Lard.

"Exactly," said Daisy Bones. "None of the children in our class has an ink pen. We all use pencils. So you can let us go at once."

The Detective Inspector was quite impressed.

"I'd like to let you all go," he said. "But there is another small matter that points to one of your classmates and it can't be a coincidence, I don't believe in them."

"What small matter?" asked Weasel.

"I believe you all went to the library before you visited the museum," said the Detective Inspector. "A page has been torn from a very old and valuable book there this morning."

"What kind of book?" asked Daisy Bones.

"*Ancient Egyptian Spells and Potions,*" said the Detective Inspector. "Page 1600."

"Does the library have another copy of the book, or know what was written on the missing page?" asked Daisy.

"No," said the Detective Inspector.

"Oh dear, this is more serious than I thought," said Daisy Bones. "I must go home at once."

"Your whole class is going home," said the Detective Inspector, "by police escort and you will all be brought back tomorrow morning for questioning. Hopefully the culprit will have owned up by then."

Chapter Four

Later that afternoon, Daisy Bones rang
Weasel and arranged to meet him at the
bus-stop at the bottom of their street.

"Where are we going, Daisy?" asked
Weasel. "I'll really catch it if my mum
finds out I've gone."

"There's a shop we need to visit."

When they got off the bus, Daisy led the way through a tangle of streets to a small alley-way with those little shops that sell knick-knacks and fake antiques. The third shop along was a tiny book store.

Inside was an untidy jumble of books.

"Hello," said the shopkeeper. "Can I help?"

"Good afternoon, do you have a book called *Ancient Egyptian Spells and Potions*?" asked Daisy Bones.

"Sure kid, I've got everything here, but it's a rare book and very expensive."

"Oh I don't want to buy it. I'd like to look at it. I need to know what's on page 1600," explained Daisy.

The shopkeeper rummaged through several boxes without success and then went to the back of the shop.

"Here it is," she said, handing it to Daisy. "It's very old, so be careful."

Daisy opened the book gently, and slowly turned the pages.

"Page 1600. To control the mind of others," she read. "Get a parrot, preferably bald, to dip a mummy's finger in cat's milk at noon on a Friday in June. Then everyone who drinks the milk will do everything you tell them to."

"Oh well, nothing to worry about then," said Weasel cheerfully.

"NOTHING TO WORRY ABOUT!" exclaimed Daisy Bones. "This is really serious. I don't want my mind controlled!"

"No chance of that," said Weasel. "It'll be hard enough for the finger thief to find a bald parrot, let alone enough cat's milk to control one whole person. I think they're on to a loser there."

"That shows how much you know," said Daisy Bones. "My nan's cockatoo plucks itself and is almost totally bald. If a cockatoo does it, I bet parrots do too!"

"OK, that's possible, but cat's milk? Let's get serious!"

"Didn't you ever hear of big cats?" asked Daisy. "It said in the paper last week that the zoo's female lion Rana had cubs. I'd say there might be a lot of cat's milk there!"

"But only a loony would go into a lion's cage and try to milk it," said Weasel.

"Exactly!" said Daisy Bones.

"Let's ring the Detective Inspector," suggested Weasel nervously.

"No point. I don't think anything will happen until just before twelve o'clock tomorrow morning at the zoo and I intend to be there to stop it!"

Chapter Five

Next morning at 8.30, the police escort arrived to take Daisy and Weasel to the museum to be questioned with the rest of their class.

They were still waiting in the lunch room at 11.15.

"I must see Detective Inspector Lard at once," Daisy told the constable on guard duty for the twentieth time.

"We will begin when everyone has arrived," said the constable.

"I must see the Detective Inspector. I think I know where the mummy's finger will be at twelve o'clock," said Daisy.

The constable sent a message and a policewoman came to the lunch room to fetch Daisy Bones and Weasel.

They were taken to a small office near the Egyptian exhibit where the Detective Inspector and the curator were waiting.

"I understand you have something to confess, Daisy Bones," said the Detective Inspector. "You do realize you are in serious trouble, don't you?"

"I'm not in trouble at all," said Daisy. "I didn't steal the mummy's finger."

"Then why did you tell the constable you know where it is?" asked the curator.

"I don't know where it is. I know where it *might* be today. The thief will probably take it to the zoo. In fact if we don't hurry we'll be too late."

"Sergeant," called the Detective Inspector. "We need a fast car to take us to the zoo immediately."

Chapter Six

The car sped along the streets towards the zoo with its siren screeching.

"Inspector, the constable told us someone from our class hadn't arrived. I didn't notice anyone missing. Who were you waiting for?" asked Daisy Bones, as they pulled up outside the zoo.

"A boy called Adam Parrot, according to my list."

"Adam Parrot!" exclaimed Daisy. "Of course."

"What's Adam Parrot got to do with anything?" asked Weasel.

"A parrot, preferably bald. Adam Parrot had that nasty accident with his chemistry set and burned off most of his hair," said Daisy. "He must be the thief! He plans to dip the stolen mummy's finger in the cat's milk!"

"Cat's milk? A bald parrot? I don't understand," said Detective Inspector Lard.

"Quick, let's get to the big cat enclosure," said Daisy Bones.

As they ran, Weasel told the Inspector about the list of ingredients they'd discovered for the mind control potion in the book.

At the big cat enclosure, the lions were lazing in the sun. Daisy hurried towards a keeper with a wheelbarrow.

"Has anyone been in there today trying to milk a lion?" she asked.

"Is this some kind of joke?" asked the keeper.

"No," said Daisy Bones. "I'm looking for a nearly bald boy called Adam Parrot. He has a mummy's finger and needs to milk a big cat."

"Is this the telly programme with that bloke hiding around the corner with a

microphone and a hidden camera?" asked the keeper, looking all around. Then he suddenly launched into a song "for the hidden camera".

The Detective Inspector and Weasel caught up with Daisy and overtook her.

"This way," called Weasel. "The mother lion got fed up with the cubs fighting at feeding time, so they are being bottle-fed with her milk in a special enclosure."

The cubs were being given their bottles. The smallest cub was playing with hers while she waited to be fed. She was holding it in her big front paws. Suddenly a hand reached in through the bars and snatched the bottle from her.

"Roarrr!" she growled.

"Follow that bottle," said Daisy Bones, dashing round to the other side of the cage and confronting the thief.

"Mrs Hoskins!" gasped Daisy and Weasel together.

Chapter Seven

Mrs Hoskins held the bottle of lion's milk in one hand and Adam Parrot's earlobe in the other.

"Take the mummy's finger out of my cardigan pocket, Adam," she commanded.

"I don't want to, Miss," whined Adam.

She squeezed his ear hard, making him yelp.

"All right, I'll do it," he gasped, reaching into her pocket.

"The game's up, Mrs Hoskins," said Daisy Bones. "Hand over that Parrot."

"Never!" said Mrs Hoskins.

Adam Parrot pulled the mummy's finger out of her pocket.

"Dip it in the milk," she said.

Suddenly, Daisy Bones sprang forward. She knocked the mummy's finger out of Adam's hand. At the same time, Weasel grabbed the cat's milk from Mrs Hoskins and, because he wasn't sure what to do next, he drank it!

43

The mummy's finger rolled across the concrete, through the bars and into the mouth of a yawning lion cub.

"Hooray for Daisy Bones!" cried the police.

"I only wanted to make the children learn," wailed Mrs Hoskins as she was led away. "Mind control is the only way to make anything stay in their brains. Otherwise it all goes in one ear and out the other."

"That was a really exciting case, Daisy," said Weasel, when they arrived home.

"When did you realize it was Mrs Hoskins?"

"I had my suspicions when I saw the ink on the mummy's hand, because Mrs Hoskins always uses a fountain pen, but for a while there I really thought it was Adam Parrot. Weasel, why do you keep licking your fingers?"

"Dunno. Ever since I drank that cat's milk I've wanted to lick my hands clean and I keep thinking about a nice, warm fire and pilchards!"

"That's strange," said Daisy Bones.

"I know and I keep wanting to... Daisy, where are you going?"

"Well, Mr and Mrs Turner are on holiday, but I'm sure I can see something moving in their house. I think I'd better investigate," said Daisy Bones.

Look out for more titles in the Red Storybooks series:

Bad Manners Day by Herbie Brennan

"Now Martha, what are we going to do about these rude boys?" asks the Queen. Martha suggests a National Bad Manners Day, and they both eagerly await the special day.

Dinosaur Robbers by Jeremy Strong

Tyrannosaurus and Triceratops may look real, but they're actually two robotic dinosaurs invented by Max's dad. However, Buster's and Binbag's beady eyes spy the dinosaurs and decide they'll come in handy for a spot of burglary …

The Magic Sponge by Michael Coleman

Is Barry Biggs ever going to get on the school football team? It's not much fun always standing on the touchline with Mr Simkin's bucket of water and sponges. But then Barry discovers Captain Tripp's *magic* sponge and thinks his big chance to be a star player has come at last.

The Twitches' Bathday by Roy Apps

It's Gert and Lil's one hundred and fourteenth birthday. It's also their *bathday*, the one day of the year when witches are supposed to have a bath. But the twitches will do *anything* to avoid having a wash, even paying a visit to the Queen …

Storybooks are available from your local bookshop or can be ordered direct from the publishers. For more information about Storybooks, write to: *The Sales Department, Macdonald Young Books, 61 Western Road, Hove, East Sussex, BN3 1JD.*